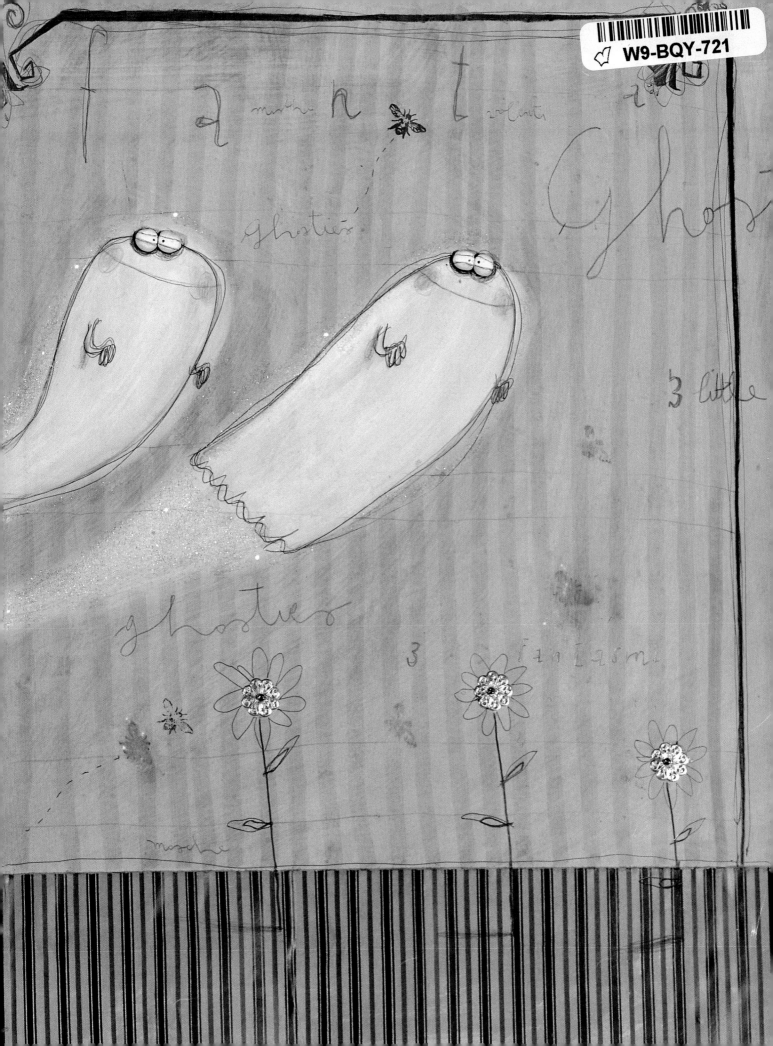

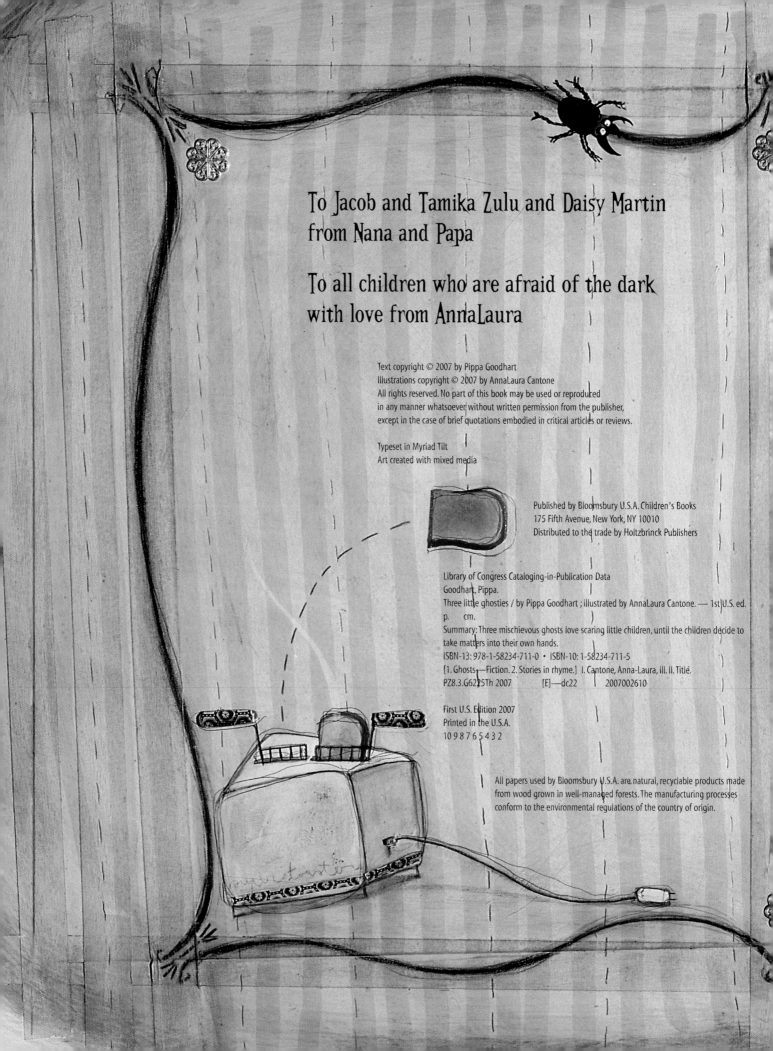

To Jacob and Tamika Zulu and Daisy Martin
from Nana and Papa

To all children who are afraid of the dark
with love from AnnaLaura

Text copyright © 2007 by Pippa Goodhart
Illustrations copyright © 2007 by AnnaLaura Cantone

Typeset in Myriad Tilt
Art created with mixed media

Published by Bloomsbury U.S.A. Children's Books
175 Fifth Avenue, New York, NY 10010
Distributed to the trade by Holtzbrinck Publishers

Library of Congress Cataloging-in-Publication Data
Goodhart, Pippa.
Three little ghosties / by Pippa Goodhart ; illustrated by AnnaLaura Cantone. — 1st U.S. ed.
p.   cm.
Summary: Three mischievous ghosts love scaring little children, until the children decide to
take matters into their own hands.
ISBN-13: 978-1-58234-711-0 • ISBN-10: 1-58234-711-5
[1. Ghosts—Fiction. 2. Stories in rhyme.] I. Cantone, Anna-Laura, ill. II. Title.
PZ8.3.G6225Th 2007   [E]—dc22   2007002610

First U.S. Edition 2007
Printed in the U.S.A.
10 9 8 7 6 5 4 3 2

Three Little Ghosties

by Pippa Goodhart

illustrated by AnnaLaura Cantone

BLOOMSBURY
CHILDREN'S
BOOKS

Three little ghosties
sat on their posties,
eating burnt toasties,
telling big boasties.

"And they all dropped their booksies
with silly frightened looksies,
then ran away home to bed."

"Hee, hee, hee," laughed the three little ghosties.

"Well," said Ghostie Number Two,
"I scared some mean witches,
sitting in dark ditches,
lipsticking their lipses,
plotting evil trickses.

"And they jumped with the frighties,
then flew off in their nighties
to hide in the deep dark wood."

"Hee, hee, hee," laughed the three little ghosties.

Ghostie Number Three said,
"I scared a huge ogre,
as big as six treeses,
standing in the breezes,
picking at his fleases.

I spooked
him with a

moan,

groan,

BOOO!!"

"He galumphed
through the woodses,
the fastest that
he couldses.

'I want my mommy,'
he said."

"Hee, hee, hee," laughed the three little ghosties.

Then the three little ghosties,
all sitting on their posties,
had finished their burnt toasties.

Said Ghostie Number One,
"Now what shall we do for a bit of fun?
Let's go haunting and scare some girlsies!"

"Yeah,
and
boyses
too!"

So they flew off their posties
and came **wailing,**

sailing, flailing

down to my house.

"woooo,

Woooo,

woooo!"

They ghostie-slither-slid
through the window cracksies
and creak-pushed
open my door.

They thought I was asleep,
so they started to creep,
Creepy,
creepy,
whisper,
whisper,

...I sat up in bed and shouted,

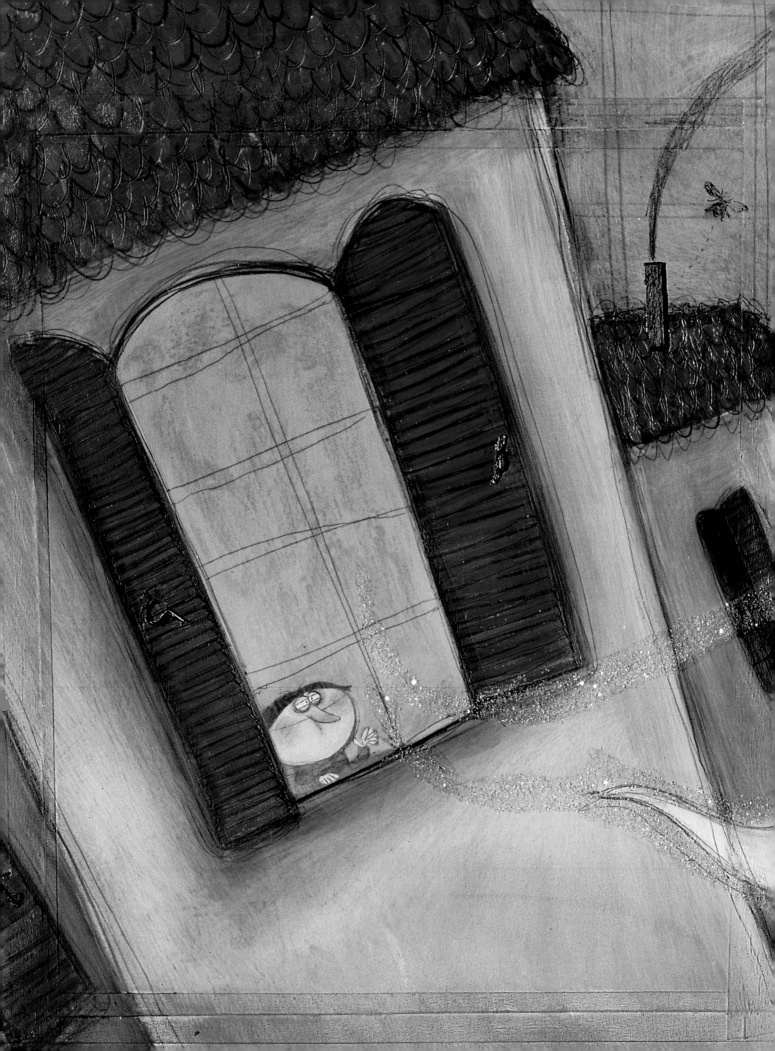

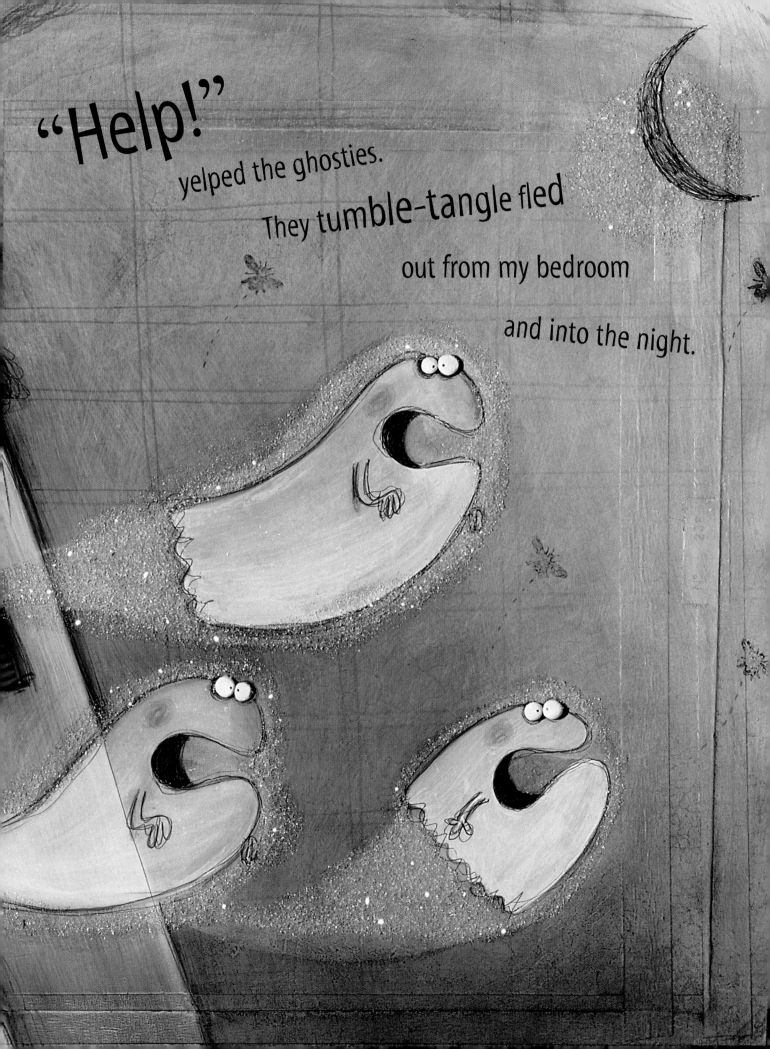

"Help!" yelped the ghosties.
They tumble-tangle fled
out from my bedroom
and into the night.

Quivering like jellies,
those three little ghosties

wobbled to their posties,

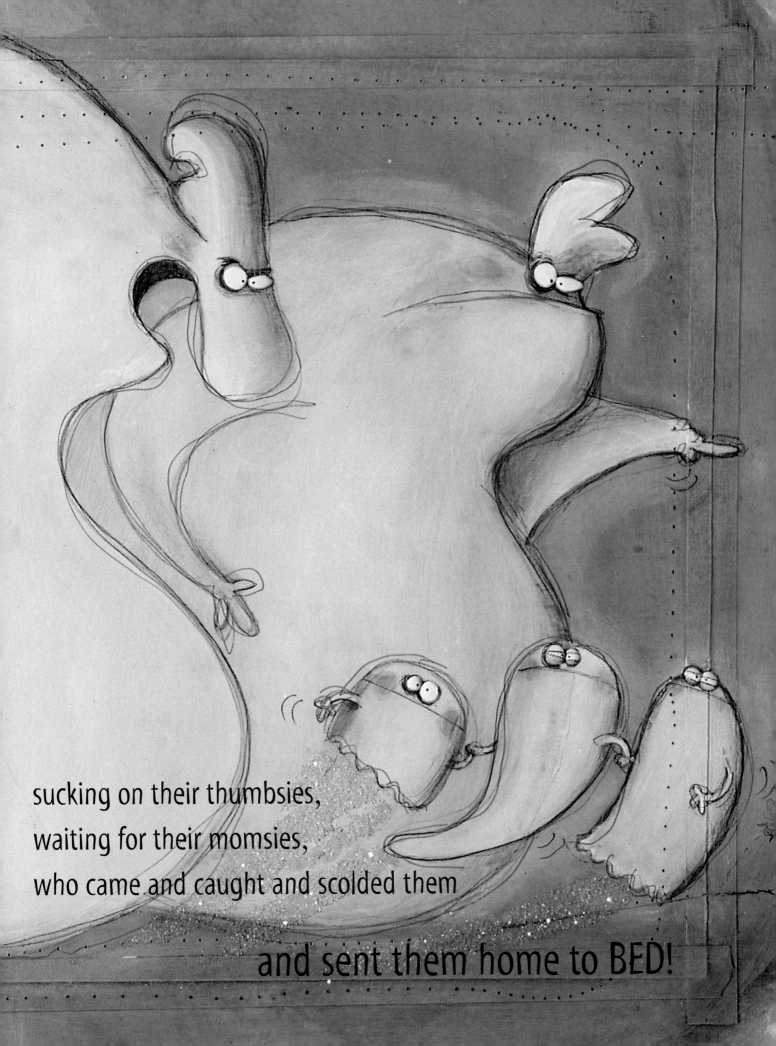

sucking on their thumbsies,
waiting for their momsies,
who came and caught and scolded them

and sent them home to BED!